Ponty The Pit Pony

Lyn Whitby

**Illustrations by
Amy Goddard**

Published by Curriculum Concepts UK Ltd – 2009

ISBN 9781906373849

Printed and bound in the UK

Dedicated to Trelewis Primary School.
The school that inspired the story.

Ponty The Pit Pony

by Lyn Whitby

Illustrations by Amy Goddard

Ponty The Pit Pony

It was darker than the darkest night. As dark as black velvet, as black as coal. Sarah couldn't see her hand in front of her face, it was creepy and so quiet too. She giggled nervously and reached out to touch the person nearest to her.

'Be careful, you nearly poked me in the eye,' said a grumpy voice that sounded like Emily.

The silence was broken. Everyone began talking and laughing at once. Some of the boys made ghostly sighs and groans and one of the girls screamed.

'Quiet please,' said Mrs Davies.

'You'd better put your lamps on again,' said the miner who was their guide. He had told them to turn off their lamps for a minute to see how dark it really was.

They were doing 'Children Underground' as part of a history project and their teacher had taken them to Big Pit Mining Museum in Blaenavon so that they could get an idea of what it was like underground in a real coal mine.

Sarah was glad when they put the lamps on again. They were on the helmets they were wearing. They all had heavy safety packs around their waists too and had to mind their heads and walk bent over for part of the way. It was cold and damp in the tunnels. There was water running down the walls in some places, and the miner kept telling them about rats and gas and cave-ins where miners were trapped for hours. Sarah shivered when she thought about it.

The best part was the stables. There must have been lots of ponies working down there. Their names were written above the stable doors. Sarah remembered some of them … Welsh, Prince, Dragon and Victor. There were others too whose names she couldn't remember. She wondered how they got down there and if they ever came up to the light and did they mind the dark and the damp and the dust.

Of course, it was boring really, Sarah thought. No one was actually working, just a lot of empty tunnels. A bit scary though. She was glad there were no cave-ins while she was there.

Later that day, back in school Mrs Davies spoke to the class.

'Well, I hope you learned something today. Now I want you all to go home and think up a good idea for a project based on your experience from today's trip.'

Sarah sighed, she detested school. History was horrible, Arithmetic was awful, Science stank, Writing was rubbish and Reading was really boring! Now she had to find a project to do but she just couldn't think of anything. All her friends seemed to have really good ideas and Sarah was worried that she wouldn't be able to do it. She felt left out and rather stupid.

'You think yourself lucky you can go to school!' Dad would say. 'Your great, great (how many times great was it?) grandmother had to work down the mines at your age!'

'I'd rather work down a mine than go to rotten school,' Sarah would mutter to herself as she flounced out of the house and dragged her feet all the way to the beastly place. Of course, she knew as she said it that it was a silly thing to say but she would never admit it.

Sarah often wondered about her great, great grandmother. She had been called Sarah too and she had lived in the same house as Sarah lived in now. The house had been much smaller then. It was part of a row of cottages and Sarah's dad had bought the one next door and knocked the two into one. He had also built an extension so that Mam had a nice big kitchen and converted the attic into one big room to make a lovely bedroom for Sarah.

The garden was a picture, not very big but there was just enough room for a swing in one corner and Sarah spent many happy hours swinging to and fro.

From the swing she could see the new school which had been built on the other side of the railway line on a slight hill. You had to go over quite a steep bridge to reach it. Sometimes seeing the other children crossing it would remind her that it was getting late and time to make her way to school. This always made her feel sad or angry and she wished she could stay on the swing all day.

At last, for today, school was out and Sarah was free to run home back to her tea and then out to the swing. But as she was swinging to and fro she found herself thinking about those children down there in the dark.

It's only words, thought Sarah, it isn't like being there. I wish I could understand what it was really like. It is so hard to imagine being in the dark when the sun is shining and the birds are singing in the trees. I'll never be able to think of an interesting project. The others are so much better at that than me.

At that point her mother called her. It was bedtime.

****

The next day was very misty. 'It will be hot later on,' said Mam.

Mam walked with her to the bottom of the bridge and Sarah started to climb the steps. It was like walking in a cloud, you couldn't see the school at all but she wasn't worried, you couldn't get lost because the bridge only went to the school, nowhere else. On the way up she met Tracy and Darren but they ran on ahead.

Sarah always walked slowly to school, half hoping she'd never get there. Then Ann and William caught up with her. They were both younger than she was.

'Oh, Sarah, we don't like this mist,' said Ann. 'We can't see where we are going. It's scary. We'll get lost.'

'Don't be silly,' said Sarah. Little children were such a nuisance. But they wouldn't leave her.

'We really hate school,' said William. 'We don't want to go today.'

Ann nodded in agreement.

'You should be glad you don't have to work down a coal mine where it is always dark and cold,' Sarah told them sternly and started to walk on quickly. I sound like my dad, she thought. Ann and William followed her closely.

It suddenly seemed that the mist instead of getting thinner was getting thicker and thicker. It was more like a fog now and they could hardly see each other at all. Then the sound of their feet on the bridge was strangely different, not that slightly echoing metallic sound but a soft, scrunchy, gravelly sound.

Just as suddenly Sarah felt that there were lots more people around them. Shadowy shapes that loomed into sight and then faded away again. Not other children … they were too big … grown-ups. She shivered and then shook herself and told herself not to be so silly, they must be nearly there by now.

That was when the fog started to thin again. It

swirled away in grey strands and through it they began to see … not the school but … what?

It was a grey and black scene, dirty buildings, gravel and dust on the floor and then looming ahead of them the black, stark pithead, tall and threatening and ever closer. Sarah stopped.

'Watch yourself!' said a gruff voice, 'I nearly tripped over you then. Come on get a move on or you'll be late for your shift.'

The man walked on past her and Sarah looked around. There were crowds of people all walking towards the pithead. There were Ann and William, at least, they looked a bit like Ann and William but smaller and dirtier and more scared than before.

'Oh, Sarah, we don't want to go down there again

today,' Ann whispered.

Sarah couldn't think of anything to say.

They were just being carried along with the crowd, nearer and nearer to the huge metal tower. The doors of the cage opened and they found themselves packed into the lift hurtling down hundreds of feet into the darkness below. Everyone was squashed in tight and it was very smelly. The black walls of the mine rushed past them; Sarah felt as if her stomach had got left behind.

The cage stopped with a bump at the bottom and everyone piled out. One or two of the miners had lamps, but most had candles. Some of the children, and there were quite a few, had nothing. Ann was sobbing quietly and William looked pale. A miner took each of them by the hand and led them away down the tunnels, grumbling gruff words of comfort as they went.

'Come on, Sarah,' said a voice. 'I'll walk you down to your section. Watch your head just here.' Sarah couldn't do anything else but follow.

It wasn't really like Big Pit at all. Well it was and it wasn't. It was dark and dusty and she remembered the water dripping down the walls but it wasn't a bit quiet. She could hear the rustle and scurry of tiny feet …could that be the rats?…

'Out of the way, girl,' shouted the miner who was leading her. 'Forgotten what happened to Robert already, have you? You'll have to step quicker than that when you're on your own or you'll end up crippled like him.'

The miner had pulled Sarah to the side of the tunnel just in time as the heavy trucks rolled past them with inches to spare. Sarah shook and trembled, remembering the stories Mrs Davies had told them about people injured by the heavy trucks full of coal that hurtled down the tunnels.

'Come on, girl, pull yourself together now,' the man said, not unkindly, 'you're all right this time. Just got to keep your wits about you, that's all. Here you are, this is your section.'

They had arrived at a large pair of double doors and they pushed through them. On the other side was a long gap and then another set of doors. Sarah remembered that this was something to do with keeping the air fresh in the tunnels.

'Now, remember what you have to do? Just open and close the doors for the drams to come through. They come slow through here so no need to worry but don't you go off to sleep now because Dai Morgan is on this roadway today and he eats little girls like you for breakfast if he finds them sleeping!' The miner laughed to himself and started to walk away.

'Where are Ann and William?' asked Sarah.

'Who?' asked the miner.

'Two small children who came down with us.'

'The Evans children, do you mean? They are small so Ann will be on the doors like you, I expect. They may put William with the ponies today. When you are all bigger we'll find other things for you to do.'

The miner started off towards the second set of doors and Sarah suddenly realised that he had the candle with him.

'Where's my candle?' she asked, looking around.

'Your candle?' asked the miner laughing 'You should have brought one with you from home. We can't afford candles for the likes of you! Not going anywhere, are you? Just sit there! You'll get light enough when the men and ponies come through. Listen well now! They don't like to be kept waiting.'

Sarah sat against the wall in the middle of her section where she was told and he left, plodding on down the tunnel. As he went through the doors and they closed behind him the darkness closed around Sarah and she thought of that moment in Big Pit when the miner had told them to turn their lamps out. She hadn't really been scared then because all her school friends had been giggling in the dark, and Mrs Davies' familiar voice telling them to be quiet for a minute had been quite comforting. Even when they were quieter she had been able to reach out and touch someone. This was different.

Sarah was quite alone. It was so dark she thought she might as well be blind. Perhaps her eyes would get used to it. But she knew they wouldn't. She started to feel very strange as though she couldn't breathe. She wanted to call out, she wanted to cry. She started to feel the tears running down her cheeks and she was sobbing. This was no good. She mustn't panic. What was it Mam-gu always said? 'What can't be cured must be endured.' She rubbed her eyes angrily and took some deep breaths. She would have to find other ways of finding her way around. What could she do? In Blindman's Buff you had to feel your way. Perhaps she could try that.

It was horrible trying to feel the way. The rock was hard and jagged and very dusty and dirty. Sarah stood up and faced the wall where she had been sitting and keeping her hands on the wall she sidestepped until she reached the doors at one end of the tunnel. It seemed to take ages.

'How can I be quick when I can't see?' wondered Sarah. 'I'll have to practise a bit.'

Still keeping her hands on the wall in front of her, she carefully sidestepped back the other way until she reached the other set of doors, this time counting her steps.

She scraped her hands on the rocky wall and once she bumped her head where the roof came down low, but she swallowed down the tears that threatened to come back and said to herself, 'At least I know where I am!'

She bravely went back in the same way to the first set of doors, checking her counting and then back once more to the second set. Then she counted herself into the middle of the section and sat down again to wait.

Waiting was hard. Sarah had never felt so lonely. Sometimes in the garden at home she had enjoyed being alone. Just watching the bees on the lavender or swinging, she hadn't wanted anyone else to be there, but she wanted someone now. Dad or Mam or Mrs Davies or even Ann and William.

What about poor little Ann? Was she in a dark section of tunnel like this waiting to rush through the blackness to open the gates? Would she be able to work out where the doors were like Sarah had? Sarah wished she had been kinder to Ann, she could have shown her what to do. Silly! She hadn't known they were going to end up here! She had been on the way to school! What had happened then? Was it the fog?

Just then she heard an almighty rumbling and clanking sound and a loud voice shouted 'Doors!' Sarah jumped to her feet bumping her head again and scraping her arm. She stopped herself rushing into the dark and carefully counted her steps to the door. It was very heavy and as she opened it a light shone through, it should have been welcome but at first it just hurt her eyes and she had to put her hand up to shield them.

'Too slow, girl. You'll have to buck up your ideas if you want your full wages this week,' said a grumpy voice. 'Come on, don't just stand there. Get these doors closed and open the next lot.

Sarah started down the tunnel. She could see now with the lamp and didn't need to count.

'Didn't you hear me? Close these first! You trying to suffocate us all or something?'

Sarah realising her mistake went back to close the first set of doors and then opened the others.

'And you make sure you close these properly before you sit yourself down again,' said the grumpy man and he started off again. The pony strained to get started and the trucks slowly moved through the doors and disappeared into the tunnel beyond.

It was dark again. Sarah closed the doors carefully. She wasn't sure what would happen if she didn't but she was afraid of explosions and gas and all those other things Mrs Davies and the miners at Big Pit had talked about and she shivered. When she had closed them she counted her way back to her spot and sat down again.

'I wonder what the pony's name was,' Sarah said to herself. 'He looked so small to be pulling those heavy trucks. He didn't look thin but his coat was smeared with coal dust and his eyes were bloodshot and tired. He sounded a bit wheezy too. I hope he is all right.'

'Will I ever see Mrs Davies again?' she wondered. 'Am I going to be working in a coalmine instead of going to school for ever and ever?'

Sarah thought of all the times she had wished it. All the silly things she had said and she started to cry again, this time in earnest.

Sarah must have cried herself to sleep and fortunately Dai the grumpy miner didn't come back that way. When she woke she had to remind herself where she was. She was hungry. She usually took a packed lunch with her to school and she had it with her in the section. She felt around for it and in a little while she found it near where she was sitting. It felt different though; and when she opened it she found, not the ham and salad sandwiches, fruit juice and cake, that her mother had packed for her, but just a dry piece of bread with a scraping of jam and a chunk of hard cheese. There was a little bottle of water to drink and nothing else. Sarah forced herself to eat it because she was so hungry but there wasn't really enough of it anyway.

The day wore on. Sarah had lost all idea of time. She had to open the doors several times more in each direction in the dark and then one of the miners gave her a stump of candle.

'Can't have you in the dark all day,' he said kindly.

'Remember to bring one with you tomorrow.'

Tomorrow, she thought, I hope I'm not here tomorrow!

The candle made such a difference. In its flickering light she could see the water running down the walls and the black beetles scurrying here and there. There were the rats too. They seemed very interested in Sarah's lunchbox. She was glad it was empty now.

'I wonder if it would be better not to be able to see them,' she said to herself, but she knew she would rather have the candle than be without it. Now she wouldn't need to count.

She saw no one else for ages and had nothing else to do but sit. She must have slept again because the next thing she knew, the miner who had taken her to her section was shaking her awake.

'Sarah, we need your help over at the stables, we're short-handed today,' he said.

'What about the doors?' she asked.

'Ann will take over here,' he replied.

Sarah looked at Ann. She was so small and frightened that Sarah felt really sorry for her.

'Do you have a candle?' she asked her.

Ann looked at her with tears in her eyes.

'It's burnt out,' she said, 'and I'm so afraid of the dark.'

Sarah gulped and said, 'Here have mine, it should

last a bit longer.'

That was the hardest thing I ever did, she thought to herself as she followed the miner back up the tunnels.

'That was a kind thing to do,' said the miner in a gentle voice, 'but don't worry, you'll have a lamp to take the pony where he's needed so it won't be too bad.'

They soon got to the stables. William was there and he had the pony ready.

'His name is Ponty,' he said, 'and he's a good worker.'

The pony was one of the smallest in the stables. A Welsh mountain pony. His coat was a lovely chestnut brown colour although it was very dusty from the coal. He whinnied when he saw Sarah and snuzzled his nose into her side.

'He hopes you've got a carrot or something for him,' said William.

'I'm sorry, I haven't got anything,' said Sarah.
'Don't worry, he's well fed.' said William 'Better than some of us, I'd say,' he added. 'Take his leading rope. Here under his chin like that. Now if you walk ahead he'll follow'.

Sarah had never led a pony before but it didn't sound too difficult.

'Here's your lamp,' said William. 'For goodness' sake take care of it. If you break it or lose it you'll really be in trouble.'

The lamp had mesh around the flame and a handle

to carry it.

'Give her a candle,' said another man. 'What's she need a lamp for?'

'It's safer where she's going,' said William. 'Mr Thomas said she's to have it.'

'Where do I have to go?' Sarah asked.

The miner told her the way. It sounded complicated but she thought it would be O.K.

'Hurry up about it,' he said, 'they're waiting for him.'

Sarah set off up the tunnel. She had the lamp in one hand and the pony's rope in the other. She liked the feel and smell of the little pony as he trotted beside her. He was good company. Every now and then he snorted and it seemed as though he was trying to talk to her. She found herself telling him all about what had happened to her that day.

'I must be mad,' she said to him, 'I know you can't understand me.'

Ponty whinnied again and Sarah smiled. This was

better than horrible tunnels and heavy doors. Then they reached a fork in the tunnel and Sarah wasn't sure which way to go.

'Now what do I do?' she asked Ponty doubtfully. 'Right or left?'

Ponty whinnied loudly and shook his head, he seemed to know the way. He turned left and quickened his pace almost pulling the rope out of Sarah's hand.

'Slow down, Ponty,' Sarah cried out. He was pulling her along so fast that she stumbled and nearly fell. She grazed her elbow on the rough wall and bumped her head but she couldn't make Ponty slow down. Then – disaster – she dropped the precious lamp and heard it roll back down the tunnel the way they had come. What would they say when she went back if she couldn't find it?

Ponty trotted on faster and faster. It seemed to be getting lighter. Where were they going? All of a sudden they were outside! They had walked out of the mine by a long steep tunnel that came out on to the mountain behind. They were in a grassy field surrounded by beautiful white hawthorn hedges. The sun was just beginning to go down and everything had a lovely, rosy glow. The difference after the mine was amazing. It was like stepping into another world.

Ponty gave another shake of his head and pulled himself free. He galloped across the field kicking up his heels. Round and round the field he went as though he would never stop.

'Ponty, Ponty,' cried Sarah. 'Come back, we'll get into terrible trouble!'

But the little pony was having the time of his life. He was galloping for sheer joy. He was free! He rolled in the grass and then he was off again.

Sarah tried to catch him. He stood still and looked at her when she called his name, but as soon as she was close enough to grab his rope he kicked up his heels, shook his head and galloped away.

He's teasing me. I'll try to sneak up on him, thought Sarah, and she waited until he stood still again. But he could see her out of the corner of his eye and he was off. Sarah tried and tried to catch him but he was too quick for her. Once she fell over and he came right up to her and nuzzled her as if to see if she was hurt but as soon as she was on her feet he dodged her and galloped to the other side of the field.

It was starting to get dark now. A pearly, grey light had replaced the rosy glow. Ponty was further away than ever. What would happen if she never caught him? Could she go back without him and explain? She didn't think she'd have the courage. They would be so angry.

'What am I going to do?' Sarah said aloud in despair.

'Talking to yourself, are you?' said a voice behind her.

Sarah jumped and turned around. There at the gate was a boy. He was older than Sarah and he held a stick in his hand. He opened the gate and came towards her walking with a limp.

'You're Sarah, aren't you?' he said 'Don't you remember me? I'm Robert.'

'Oh,' said Sarah. Then she remembered that Robert had been injured in the mine. She wondered what he did now. She couldn't help looking at his twisted leg.

Robert seemed to guess what she was thinking.

'I was lucky,' he said. 'After the accident they took me on at the Lewis farm. I'm good with horses you see. I've been there ever since.'

'What's the matter with Ponty?' she asked him. 'I can't get him to come back.'

'Nothing wrong with him,' said Robert. 'Look at him he's having a wonderful time. Don't worry, I'll get him back for you.'

Robert went slowly back to the gate and out into the lane.

'Back in a minute.' he said over his shoulder.

Sarah sat down on the grass. It was true, Ponty was having a wonderful time. He had stopped galloping around and was quietly grazing. He looked so content. Sarah smiled at him.

He shouldn't have to go back, she thought. He's so happy here. But what will happen to me if he doesn't?

Sarah sat watching him for what seemed a long while. She was getting more and more worried with every passing minute. What if Robert didn't come back? She found she couldn't sit still any more, she got up and started walking back and forth, rubbing her hands together.

But eventually he did come. He had some carrots with him. He whistled softly to Ponty and held out the carrots.

Ponty lifted his head and looked at him and very slowly came across the field. Robert gently took the rope and talked to him in a soft voice.

How did you do that?' asked Sarah. She was relieved but also rather cross that Robert had made it look so easy.

'I told you I have a way with horses, didn't I? I'll come back with you, Sarah,' he said. 'Look, he trusts me.'

'I wish he could stay out here,' said Sarah sadly. 'It must be horrible for him in that mine all the time.'

'He has to work for his living the same as we do,' said Robert. 'And he's well fed and well cared for. Better than some I've seen.'

At least he's had a bit of a day off, thought Sarah. Then she remembered the lamp.

'I've lost the lamp they gave me,' she said 'What can I do?'

'Was it a Davy lamp?' asked Robert.

'Yes, I think so,' said Sarah, trying to remember what they had learned in class about the different lamps they used.

'You'll be in big trouble if we don't find it,' said Robert. 'Let's hope it's near the entrance to the tunnel or we'll have to go back in the dark. I've got a few matches on me but no candle.'

Robert led the way back down the tunnel. Ponty following on with no fuss at all. As they walked it got darker and darker. Robert used some of his matches, shaking them out just before they burnt his fingers. They strained to see, looking in every dark corner. Robert's matches were nearly all used.

'We'll never find it, it's so dark and there are so many rocks and crevices. We could look for ever and never see it!' Sarah said. Her voice trembled and she shivered.

'Don't give up,' said Robert. 'It must be here somewhere.' At that moment her foot struck something. Was it just another stone? No, it was the lamp! Sarah gasped with relief.

'A bit battered, I'm afraid,' said Robert looking at it, 'but it will still light.'

'Oh dear,' said Sarah. 'Will they be cross? They told me specially to look after it.'

'No use worrying about that,' said Robert. 'Let's get Ponty back and we'll see.'

'Look at the state of this lamp!' shouted one of the miners, as soon as they got back.

He towered over Sarah, scowling down at her, his big face red with anger. Ponty bridled and tried to pull away when he saw him. The pony's ears were flat and his eyes rolled. He's afraid of that man, thought Sarah.

'And we've wasted nearly a whole shift waiting for that horse,' he went on. 'A good beating is what you need, girl.'

He grabbed Sarah's wrist with one hand and with the other he reached for a leather strap that was hanging on the wall.

Sarah couldn't believe that this was happening. No one had ever hit her before. The worst Dad did was to stop her pocket money and Mam just shouted when she was really cross. She felt her knees go wobbly. She thought she was going to faint. The man lifted the strap. Sarah cowered and tried to free herself – then Robert stepped in between them.

'Always were handy with the strap weren't you, Owain Rees?' he said. 'Leave the girl alone. It isn't her fault.'

'You want some too, do you?' said the miner lifting the strap again, this time to hit Robert.

'What's going on here?' said a voice. It was the kind miner who had given Sarah the candle.

'This girl deserves a good thrashing. She's damaged a lamp and disappeared for half a shift with a valuable pony.'

'I couldn't help it,' said Sarah trembling. She couldn't blame Ponty, she didn't want the nasty miner to turn on him and thrash him instead. 'I just got lost, that's all,' she said. Well, that was true!

The kind miner looked at Robert, then at Ponty. Had he guessed what had happened? He seemed to be in charge here because the next thing he said was,

'Leave it, Owain. I agree she couldn't help it.' Then softly, as if to himself, he added, 'Ponty always did have a mind of his own, didn't you, boy?' He gently scratched Ponty's nose.

Ponty whinnied and nodded, then walked determinedly into his stall and started pulling hay from his haynet.

'We want the girl fit to work tomorrow, don't we?' he went on aloud, 'you beat her and she'll be no use to us at all.'

Owain growled at him but he put down the strap and let Sarah go. She sank to the floor in tears.

'Shift's over boys. What are we doing down here?' someone said. 'Leave Ponty to his supper and let's get above ground.'

Robert helped Sarah to her feet.

'Come on,' he said sympathetically, 'let's go.'

Sarah gulped back her tears but she couldn't stop sobbing. She wiped her face as best she could on her sleeve. She didn't have a handkerchief.

They walked back together joining others along the way and crowded into the cage. In a few minutes they were back on top, but not to sunshine. The day was over. Sarah had been working for 12 hours and it was nearly dark.

She said goodbye and thank you to Robert and followed the crowd of workers back down to the village because there didn't seem anything else to do. Perhaps on the way down she would suddenly find herself back on the bridge and on her way home from school … but no! She was in the same village she had left that morning – but what a change.

It was a dirty, grimy village street. Everything black with coal dust. All the new houses had disappeared and the row of cottages where she lived looked small and mean. The curtains were thin and poor and there was no garden to speak of, just a grimy vegetable patch.

'Come in, Sarah, you must be tired.' The woman who greeted her looked a bit like her mother but she wore shabby clothes and looked sad and careworn. If she noticed Sarah's tear-stained face she made no comment. 'Your turn for the tub after your brothers.'

After Sarah's bath in an iron tub in front of the fire in water that didn't seem very clean, she was given a sort of soup with bread and bundled off to bed. Not to her own big attic room though, with the quilt and carpet and TV, but to a small room at the back of the cottage where she shared a bed with two younger sisters. The sheets were clean but worn and the blanket was thin.

Sarah lay awake thinking. She thought she could still feel the throb, throb, throbbing of the mine and, in the distance, singing. The voices of the men were deep and rich, the song was beautiful but somehow sad and haunting.

The two smaller children curled up close to her and she felt a sort of comfort to feel them there.

Who would have thought that she would be sharing a bed like this? Sarah fell asleep.

****

When Sarah woke up she was afraid to open her eyes in case she was still in that awful, cold, bare room she had gone to sleep in.

'Sarah, Sarah you'll be late.' came a voice.

It sounded like Mam. Oh, let it be Mam! she thought and she opened her eyes slowly.

No! She was still in the bed she had gone to sleep in. She crept out trying not to disturb the little girls who were now curled up together on the other side of the bed.

'Will this never be over?' she wondered in horror. 'How will I ever get back?'

There was nothing for it but to get up and dressed. She noticed her clothes for the first time as she put them on. She must have been too tired to think about them last night. They were shabby and thread-bare and so old-fashioned. A dark woollen dress, dirty stockings and shoes like clogs. She struggled into them, so many buttons, and slowly went downstairs.

Breakfast was a sort of thin porridge and bread. The whole family sat around the table talking. How could so many people live in such a small house? Then it was time to go to work again.

There were streams of people climbing up the slope towards the pit head and Sarah felt a wave of panic.

'I can't do this again,' she said to herself and then in horror, 'I've forgotten my candle!' but she couldn't turn back, the press of people just pushed her forward.

As Sarah climbed it became misty again, then the fog closed in and the people around her seemed to fade into shadows. Her foot hit something metal and she stumbled and put out her hand. She touched the cold metal rail of the bridge. Her heart jumped. Could she be back? Gingerly she stepped forward, her foot was on the first step. She was back on the bridge to the school!

Sarah started to run up the steps but then she thought about the clothes she was wearing.

'I can't go to school dressed like this,' she said aloud.

She looked down at herself and found that she was wearing her school uniform.

'How did that happen?' she wondered.

She felt great! She ran up the steps and over the bridge. As she went, the fog lifted and she could see the school clearly. On the end of the bridge she saw Ann and William and someone else with them. It was Robert, or was it? It looked like Robert, and he had his leg in plaster and was walking with a crutch.

Sarah stared in disbelief.

'What have you done to your leg?' she asked him anxiously. Was the past getting mixed up with the present?

'I broke it playing rugby,' he replied, 'I'm staying with Ann and William for a bit. They're my cousins, you know. My name's Daniel.'

Sarah almost laughed with relief, then, not wanting to seem rude, she said, 'I'm sorry about your leg. My name's Sarah.' They walked over the bridge to the school together.

In class that day Mrs Davies asked them all if they had decided on their project. They went round the class, everyone seemed to have a good idea and Sarah still wasn't sure if hers was good enough and what if someone else had thought of it too and said it before her. She felt nervous and a bit shy.

'Come on then, Sarah,' said Mrs Davies, 'your turn, what are you going to do?' The whole class seemed to look at Sarah expectantly.

Sarah took a deep breath and said 'I'm going to find out all I can about the ponies and write about their lives and how they worked with the children in the mines. I'm going to call it "Ponty's Day Out".'

'What a lovely idea,' said Mrs Davies and everyone agreed.

THE END

Can you find these gases in the wordsearch?

HYDROGEN   NITROGEN   METHANE
HELIUM   OXYGEN

```
O H R H N I T R O G E N
J X G Q L L S K A N Z H
Y C Y J E J G W K V Y C
S R R G X A H C T D H A
V I S C E A D K R P E N
A T Q W N N U O M X L A
P C J Y E K G A A L I N
D K B F U E Z I R T U M
L Z X L N Y Z S V B M L
C H X V E N A H T E M J
R S A R L E Y S R A N V
U R N S E A O S S K A C
```

Can you find these rocks and minerals in this wordsearch?

SANDSTONE GRANITE DIAMOND
EMERALD SILVER CHALK COAL
RUBY OPAL GOLD

```
E L Y C Y H T W Z B W M O R W E
X F L H L B N N Q L L P C E Y X
S G C A S L H Q L H A V M W V K
O P A L J B O A Z L W D L O G B
N Q J K G T O S B N P F K V K Q
U H Q M G C Q R L E B H S G C S
J E G V K Z M R T G W A I Z B I
O D N G S W D I B X R Q L G F X
G I R O U Z N L H W U Z V R L A
J A V G T A T V A L X W E U Y Z
V M W S R S R M Q R X Y R B U W
R O J G Q J D T L T E Z F Y R B
O N F J W I F N N K K M I M H D
U D I M B E R C A V U Z E W W F
```

Which are types of rock?

_____

Which are precious stones?

_____

Which are metals?

_____

Can you find the names of these ponies in the wordsearch? Cross them off as you find them.

ALBERT   DRAGON   FOSTER   VICTOR
SILVER   PRINCE   PONTY   WELSH   PAT

```
F L M R A M A I K Z H P U J T I
I J T A E G F P U J T H M R R S
T B F Y H G F E E J O A C C E D
M C B E Y V C V R J F I Y B B E
C J D M I N R E T S O F N B L V
X Q Z C I W Y O D P T R H A A N
H K T R T D F Z S R E V U Y B F
N O P F A P N P P I M R E C P S
R O S Q P O K A C B L I S Q A A
D D G Q C N C T K E Y V F I L S
L I C A W T Y J Y L I S E O P G
H B O Y R Y C J R V U B T R B Q
S K D L P D X I Q J Z M V W E C
L K E Y N C R Z P L U K S N T T
E C Q L S E J H A K L N H T J Y
W B G N P S Y Z Z G Z Z X C X P
```